Beyond Walls Of Silence

A Collection Of Short Stories With A Twist Ending.

Mystery, Crime, and Psychological Thriller Stories

Hazel Aubrell

Hazel Aubrell

Beyond the Walls of Silence

© Copyright 2020 Hazel Aubrell - All rights reserved.

The content contained within this book may not be reproduced, duplicated, or transmitted without direct written permission from the author or the publisher.

Under no circumstances will any blame or legal responsibility be held against the publisher, or author, for any damages, reparation, or monetary loss due to the information contained within this book. Either directly or indirectly.

Legal Notice:

This book is copyright protected. This book is only for personal use. You cannot amend, distribute, sell, use, quote or paraphrase any part, or the content within this book, without the author or publisher's consent.

Disclaimer Notice:

Please note the information contained within this document is for educational and entertainment purposes only. All effort has been executed to present accurate, up-to-date, and reliable, complete information. No warranties of any kind are declared or implied. Readers acknowledge that the author is not engaging in the rendering of legal, financial, medical or professional advice. The content within this book has been derived from various sources. Please consult a licensed professional before attempting any techniques outlined in this book.

By reading this document, the reader agrees that under no circumstances is the author responsible for any losses, direct or indirect, which are incurred as a result of the use of the information contained within this document, including, but not limited to, — errors, omissions, or inaccuracies.

Want free goodies?

E-mail us at:
kdp2022business@gmail.com
And we will send some free goodies your way

Beyond the Walls of Silence

TABLE OF CONTENTS

A Perfect Crime..7

My love..16

Justice..25

The Difficult Decision.....................................39

The Prophecy..52

Forever...57

Blood Lover...61

Valentine's Day...65

A Twisted End...75

Behind Every Great Man................................88

What a Hero..96

The New Revolution.......................................99

Traitors...106

The End..115

Hazel Aubrell

Dedication

To whoever is looking for something new, you are fortunate to stumble on this collection.

Enjoy.

A Perfect Crime

He took a deep breath while his body fell onto a nearby stool.

He killed her. He killed his wife; finally, he did it. He had planned this for a long time since he decided that he could no longer tolerate her constant annoyance and her ceaseless quarrels.

A whole year of planning.

At first, he convinced her to move from their neighborhood to Los Angeles's suburbs.

In their new home, which they chose at the edge of the city, he began digging in their backyard, which overlooked a deserted area, making two meters long, one-meter-wide pit and four meters deep.

When she asked him what he was doing, he convinced her that he would set up a private swimming pool. He instructed her not to tell anyone because it was a surprise to everyone, and because she loved to show off, she kept it a secret.

The only thing that bothered him during the digging process was the ants - giant, huge ants filling the soil everywhere as if they were settling in a new home before it was built -. He tried a lot to get rid of the ants and their painful stings using insecticides, burning fluids, and even gasoline, which he poured into their hole, then set it on fire.

The ants disappeared every time, but they always reappeared after a few days. In the end, he was tired of the fighting, so he decided to be satisfied by wearing some protective clothes.

The city agricultural engineer told him that it was a type of termite, resistant to regular pesticides; he promised him to bring a particular pesticide, but he did not, and he did not ask him again because he did not want to attract attention to the hole, in which his wife would settle forever.

He complained to everyone about his wife throughout that year, saying she was no longer in love with him and that he suspected her relationship with another person. After several months, he began to complain that she was threatening to leave him.

He realized that the hour of execution had come, so one night. While she was preparing dinner, he surprised her with a nylon bag on her head. He held it tightly as he pushed his body away from her to avoid her nails and kicks until her breath subsided and stopped forever.

He was sure that she took her last breath, but despite that, he kept grasping the bag with force until he realized that she couldn't survive.

Her features inside the bag were hideous and ugly, with her tongue hanging out of her mouth and her eyes widening in pain and terror.

With a trembling hand, he dropped the bag and piled it up, and he threw it into the leftover basket, then he sat panting. The essential step was done, she was killed, and the next step remained to bury her.

After putting her body in the pit, he would pour some tar on her body to ensure that her corpse's smells wouldn't leak out. After that, he would pour dirt on her. He waited few minutes to calm down before contacting everyone, her family, relatives, colleagues, friends. He asked everyone about her in horror, suggesting that he was looking for her like a madman, and there was nothing wrong with some wailing, tears, and crying.

Even that he trained himself to do it for a long time, his plan was tight and perfect.

He bought several rolls of grass from another public garden up to the pit, and he would spread them over the entire back garden. He would scatter some roses on it to not occur for anyone to look for her corpse underneath. Everything was meticulously planned, with the utmost precision. He did not leave a single detail, no matter how small it was.

He remained sitting in his seat until his breath calmed down, then he got up and brought a huge bag which he prepared in advance, a thick, strong bag. He put his wife's body in that bag for a whole hour and tightly closed it after putting many mothballs inside to ensure that the smell would not leak. He sat down to relax for some time and put his thoughts in order.

According to the plan, he spread rolls of weeds on the backyard garden floor, distributing roses and flowers at the edges, leaving only the pit. Everything must be finished quickly after burying her.

He put the tar bowl on fire near the pit, he carried his wife's body, and threw it into the pit, he cast a final glimpse on her. At that moment, she could no longer bother him nor shout at him. Her loud voice would not bother him again, and he shut her down forever.

He felt a sting in his leg while standing on the edge of the hole, he saw a large ant walking on the cuff of his pants, and he dropped it away.

"Oh, what a ridiculous ant, this is not your time at all."

He noticed a swarm of them walking at the tip of the pit; a sadistic thought occurred to him, which drove him to come back inside to bring a little alcohol, pour it on the swarm of ants, then lit it.

In enjoyment, he watched the ants burn. Nothing would defeat him, neither his wife nor the ants.

The ants burned to the end in a few moments while heating the tar in a large bowl; it flowed and became like a dark black lake. He tilted the bowl in a way he trained in before, then poured the tar on the body of his wife until he covered it completely.

At the edge of the pit, he stood watching the result of his work in admiration, the plan elaborated, the perfect crime, the crime that they claimed was impossible.

Despite him, a loud laugh came out from his lips, a victorious, confident, raging, and robust laughter.

At the edge of the hole, and while he was still carrying the shovel with his left hand, he waved his right fist into the air. At that moment, he was free, freed from his wife, from her inconvenience, and her quarrels, from the prison in which she put him, at that exact moment, he regained his freedom, and ...

Suddenly he was out of balance when the edge of the pit collapsed under his feet. He slumped, and he tried to cling to anything, but he was in the middle of an empty garden. There was nothing to cling to except the hot pot.

With an instinctive movement, he grabbed it. Still, the heat of the bowl forced him to let go, falling to the bottom next to his wife. In strange harmony, the digging shovel fell on his head and hit him at the same moment that he felt something scorching on his legs, then he lost consciousness.

He didn't know how long he was unconscious, but it was not for a long time because it was still dark out there. For him, it was just a small incident, so he would come out of the hole to continue the plan, but he was unable to move his right arm and legs. What happened? Did he hit something? He tried to raise his head and tilt his eyesight to realize what happened?

He was shocked; his legs were stuck to the tar, which he poured over the body of his wife. This part was not in the plan, and the possibility was never appreciated by his mind, but there was still hope because his left arm was free, and so was his spade.

He could use his edge to free his legs and right arm; it was only a matter of time. A mistake like this will not spoil his tight plan, but what was that pain? All over his body, he felt many painful bites, his eyes widened with horror.

From the collapsed part, he revealed a colossal cell of a giant termite, and at that moment, his whole body was covered with them. Thousands of ants on his body, stinging him mercilessly and devouring him to death.

He died an absurd death.

The End

"My love."

My heart was filled with incredible tension when I heard her voice calling me. In the past, my heart was twitching with joy whenever I heard her voice at any moment of the day.

Things change. I did not feel her as she approached me. Still, I tried to ignore her, pretending to be preoccupied with the plan that I was supposed to present to my boss early the next morning, but I could not control the increasing tension inside me; Especially when I heard her voice right behind me as she whispered:

"I missed you."

I ignored her words again, perhaps she would go and leave me alone, but she continued not bothered that I ignored her:

"You still work late."

I murmured in tension:

"I'm supposed to present this early in the morning."

She whispered in softness:

"But I'm here."

My eyebrows tied, and I said in tension mixed with some intensity:

"You always come to me without an appointment."

She replied softly:

"I come whenever I miss you."

I saw her spinning smoothly around the drawing table, bending over to catch a glimpse of the drawings. She smiled a broad smile and said:

"It looks like the mansion of our dreams."

In the past, her smile bewitched me but today.

"You still remember our dreams?"

She said it softly, I murmured, trying to get my gaze away from her:

"It was your dream."

Her voice carried a firm tone when she replied:

"Dreams can come true with a little hope."

The same words that I always heard when we were together with the same firm tone in her voice that made me feel like a student standing in front of his teacher explaining a life lesson.

"Dreams change over time."

I said it with a bit of nervousness, so she looked at me with an angry look, saying:

"It seems you don't love me anymore."

I breathed in tension and said:

"Please, I am exhausted with my work."

She gave me the same look before saying with some sharpness:

"You always promised to love me, only me."

I did not try to comment on her words; instead, I was pretending to be preoccupied with the drawing, so I tried to change the subject:

"Is this the time to talk about love?"

She replied nervously:

"All times are good for talking about love."

I said sharply:

"What about working time?"

She leaned toward me, making me more nervous, and she said:

"It's the best time to talk about love."

She was close to me in a way that made me feel cold, so I straightened to move my face away from her, and I replied:

"If my boss didn't receive this plan tomorrow morning, I might lose my job."

With an angry tone, she replied:

"It seems that you forgot that I was the one who helped you get this job, which you are refusing to give up for me today."

I was feeling very nervous whenever I looked at her in recent months, but despite this, I forced myself to look at her, and I said:

"I certainly haven't forgotten, but ..."

I didn't complete my statement when she interrupted me in anger:

"But you already forgot."

I shook my head, saying in tension and nearly bursting:

"You know that all circumstances have changed."

Her face was covered with anger, and she shouted:

"Circumstances or the heart?!"

I looked at her in silence without saying a word, so she continued sharply:

"It is Kate, isn't she?!"

I felt real disorientation, so I looked at her saying:

"She is just a co-worker."

I was terrified to look at her face when she replied:

"What a silly attempt."

I slowly turned my head, trying to look at her. Simultaneously, every atom in my being prevented me from this; even my tongue could not say anything. She added in anger:

"You sometimes forget that I can see the truth."

Once again, my tongue could not speak, so she turned around me with the same softness, saying:

"Your way of dealing with her, your dreamy looks, and your hot voice when you talk to her. All these things never suggest that she is just a co-worker."

I murmured in difficulty:

"In fact, I …"

She interrupted me:

"The reality is that this deceiving person has taken advantage of my absence to become close, to put her nets around you, to trap you, and to occupy my place in your heart."

I murmured nervously:

"Don't call her a deceiving person."

She exclaimed:

"You see?!"

Once again, she looked at my face without answering. I knew that she would spot my lie no matter what I said or did. Still, I could not tell her the truth because I was already immersed in love with Kate. I was really drenched in the love of her tenderness and simplicity; I was melting when I saw her sweet smile, and when I heard her gentle warm words, I just loved being with her in one room…

"You promised me that you would love no one but me."

She said it while crying, so I took a deep breath, trying to calm my nerves before murmuring:

"You know I tried."

She replied bitterly:

"Trying is not enough."

I murmured nervously:

"Our separation was not my intention; You know I didn't mean this."

She turned back while saying:

"I forget sometimes."

I took another deep breath and said:

"I have endured this for a long time, but you know that I have to go on with my life."

She gave me a sad look and asked:

"With Kate?!"

I lowered my eyes, and I muttered in tension:

"She or another one."

She paused for a while before replying:

"She is better than others."

I felt her voice moving away from me when she added:

"She was one of my best friends, at least."

I remained silent. I tried not to comment on her statement until she left, and I realized that she was no longer there.

I took another deep breath and looked at the drawing board, the same dialogue every night and the same end. I admitted that I loved her from all my being, but my life must continue. I wondered as I returned to my work:

"Would this torture ever end if I married Kate and continued my life, or would my ex-girlfriend continue her daily visits to me since she died last year??"

The End

Justice

It was a stressful day for Dr. Liam.

He examined more than fifty patients in the General Hospital because he was the head of the Department of Internal Medicine. He spent nearly two hours in the health insurance clinic, during which he examined a lot of patients. Still, it consumed the time he usually devoted to his daily rest, so he had to go directly to his private clinic.

He chose an elegant area, and he furnished it with furniture befitting his name. He provided it with the latest medical equipment and devices.

How exhausted he felt when he arrived at the clinic; at the moment he saw the crowds in the hall, he ran to the examination room, called the clinic nurse, and exclaimed in anger:

"What is this, Ethan? Didn't I tell you that I only see twenty patients a day?!"

The nurse answered calmly:

"This is their exact number; the rest are here just to accompany them."

This angered Dr. Liam but to save time, he asked Ethan to admit the first patient immediately.

For nearly three hours, he examined the patients, talked to some of them, or followed others' analyses. For a moment, it seemed to him the day would never end.

Finally, after he counted those who he examined, he realized that he was left with only one patient; he breathed a sigh of relief and said through an intercom:

"Send the last patient Ethan."

Ethan didn't answer this time, so he shouted sharply:

"The last patient!!"

The door opened immediately after his shout, and three people entered, a man, a woman, and a twenty-five-year-old man. They were clearly one family, their features were primarily the same, and from the first glance, he realized that the young man was his last patient. He was thin, pale, distracted, and the disease appeared from every glimpse of his face and body.

"Sit down and tell me what you are suffering from."

The young man sat in silence while his father murmured calmly:

"Not able to speak yet?"

These words seemed strange to Liam, so he asked:

"What do you mean by "yet"?! Does he suffer from mental retardation or what?!"

The mother answered him in sympathy:

"He is not fully developed yet."

He looked again at the young man and murmured:

"I am still incapable of understanding."

The father exchanged a silent look with the mother then said:

"We all suffer from a rare condition."

The doctor sat on his seat and asked:

"What case is this?!"

The father answered slowly:

"We are not growing normally."

The father and mother seemed very normal, which made it seem strange, so Dr. Liam slipped back in his seat more and said:

"May I have more explanation?!"

The father and mother exchanged another silent look, while the young man seemed to be lost, as if the matter did not concern him, then the mother answered:

"Our situation is different from yours, we were born in good shape, but we can't grow in the absence of those around us."

Liam smiled, or he tried to smile while saying:

"I haven't read in my whole life about something like this."

The father quickly replied:

"It has not yet been diagnosed."

It seemed to him that he was facing a group of idiots, so he decided not to engage with them in a lengthy discussion, and he pointed to the young man saying:

"Can you sit on the examination table?!"

The young man nodded positively, confirming his ability to comprehend and understand the words. As soon as the young man laid on the bed, Dr. Liam followed him, then said:

"If you can understand what I'm saying, just nod."

The young man nodded his head; his eyes looked as if they were carefully examining the doctor's face, so he patted him and then began to roll the blood pressure monitor on his arm while holding his wrist to measure his heartbeats. Suddenly the doctor's eyes widened.

The young man's pulse was very high.

He was automatically in the group of pathological conditions as he exceeded, according to the measurement of Dr. Liam's expert hand's fingers, more than six hundred beats per minute, compared to the regular pulse rates that do not exceed a hundred beats per minute.

As for measuring the blood pressure in his arm, it was more surprising that it was so low that it would not be suitable for him to be alive. With all his amazement and tension, Dr. Liam murmured:

"This young man is suffering badly."

The mother murmured while she was observing them:

"His condition was worse before he entered here."

Dr. Liam put his stethoscope on the young man's chest to listen to his heartbeats. We will not exaggerate if we say that he was dreaded because those irregular beats had never been heard before.

They did not follow the normal rhythm of any heartbeat, not only in the healthy or sick people but also in a human rate.

"The young man needs a comprehensive examination."

Said Dr. Liam in tension as he grabbed the blood pressure monitor from the young man's arm, but he was surprised at the young man holding his wrist and nodding his head forcefully.

Despite his weakness, his thin fingers were strong; it seemed like an iron hook. He gripped the doctor's wrist and prevented him from escaping; Dr. Liam felt slight dizziness as he tried to snatch his wrist from the fingers of the young man, who clung to it with force. Suddenly, the father said in strictness:

"Not now."

He barely said it, and the young man released the doctor's wrist immediately.

For some reason, Dr. Liam felt dizzy, so he constricted in difficulty as he returned to his office, and he murmured:

"You can come down from there."

The young man looked more energetic than he was. As he left the examination table, he came back to the bench opposite the doctor's office. With a big smile, the mother patted his shoulder, murmuring:

"Everything will get better."

The young man nodded, and a pale smile appeared on his lips for the first time. Dr. Liam murmured while his feeling of weakness and dizziness was increasing:

"I will send you to do some necessary medical tests as I have never seen a condition like yours before."

He wrote a long list with a vast number of tests and analyzes, the father said as he was looking at the list:

"Do you recommend a specific lab?!"

Dr. Liam tried to resist that weakness, which was increasing within him, and he answered:

"Dr. Carmen's lab is in the next apartment; I think it is still working to this hour."

The father murmured with a faint smile:

"She is your wife, isn't she?!"

Dr. Liam raised his eyes to him, looked at his face, and smiled for a moment before he answered in an apparent nervousness:

"Yes, she is my wife. Does this make any difference?!"

The mother shook her head, murmuring:

"Not for us."

While the father replied calmly:

"I was just wondering: Why do some doctors recommend laboratories that their wives own?! Doesn't that sound a little bit hypocritic?"

Dr. Liam continued the list while nervously saying:

"Why?! At least it's a lab I trust."

The father said, with some irony:

"And his profits go back to the family in all cases."

Dr. Liam suppressed his anger, diverted his face from the father's disgusting smile, and went on to complete this long list of tests and analyzes. Even if he admitted deep down that the man was right, part of what he said was correct; it was a matter of profits. Perhaps this was why half of the list he was writing contained tests and analyzes that have no value or importance and were not appropriate even with the patient's condition.

Still, a case that he had not experienced before and the clothes of these people suggest that they were wealthy enough to spend on a complete laboratory, why not?!

But his growing sense of weakness forced him to end this session quickly. Hence, he extended his hand with three papers, which contained the list of tests and analyses, and he said with a bit of intensity:

"You can do this in any lab you want."

He was expecting the father or the mother to pick up the three papers. Still, he was surprised by the young man grasping his wrist again with force and looking at him with surprisingly flashing eyes, he tried to pull his wrist from those steel fingers while shouting:

"Ethan, where are you?!"

With the last part of his question, he felt as if all his vitality was flowing from his body. He saw with weary eyes a big smile on the mother's lips while the father said:

"Your nurse will not respond."

He shouted louder:

"Ethan, why don't you answer ?!"

The mother answered him with a big smile:

"Because he's no longer able to."

Then she leaned forward continuing:

"Didn't I tell you that our son was worse before he got here?!"

He did not understand what she meant, but his heart was filled with great fear. He was worn out in increasing weakness, he tried to utter something, but his tongue was unable to do so, while he was surprised by the young man, whose face blushed saying vividly:

"You were right, Dad; they are not listening."

Dr. Liam was utterly worn out; he no longer could resist the young man when the father said:

"We told you that we are not like others, we can't live without their presence; you did not comprehend a single letter of what we said."

The young man, who had regained all his vitality, leaned on him as he continued:

"We said that we are not like you, human beings, we are parasitic creatures, and we cannot grow or live without absorbing the energy and vitality from your bodies. My parents' choice was you because you, in turn, are a human parasite, you don't show mercy to the sons of your kind, and you absorb their vitality without mercy so that you and your wife can live comfortably."

"I bet you that half of what you wrote wouldn't help me in anything except to increase the revenues of your wife's lab."

The mother's smile expanded more, and she added:

"Your foolish nurse was astonished when we asked him to be the last check-up in your clinic, but his astonishment was mixed with horror when our beloved son absorbed the nectar of vitality and life from his body, just as he is doing to you now and as he will do to your wife shortly after."

The father said to his son, who had regained all the vitality and energy of any young man at his age:

"A parasitic organism absorbing a parasite human, it is the justice that we have been practicing for more than ten thousand years here."

Dr. Liam did not hear the phrase's last part, for he lost all his human body's vitality. Forever.

The End

The Difficult Decision

Ashley cried for a long time that night, she had never cried like that in her life before, and she did not even imagine that she might. Since her marriage, she had dreamed of having children and becoming a mother, just as every wife or husband dreams.

Although her marriage was perfect and successful, and even though she adored her husband Michael, whom she had a love affair with throughout the college years, and they were bound after that together by the sacred bond of marriage after they graduated from the College of Sciences. Still, that marriage was missing the most crucial part in it, which was a kid.

Six years have passed since they got married without having children, but life went by, and with the passage of life, she was panicking more and more.

After their second year of marriage, both began to consult doctors, but that did not result in anything. All the examinations and analyses proved that both were 100% healthy, and there was no single obstacle preventing them from conceiving.

A doctor, whom she trusted a lot, said that the problem was not in either of them. Still, she would not be able to conceive except with minimal odds if she stayed married to Michael, and he would not be able to conceive if he remained married to her. Both would be able to conceive if they were separated, but each of them was bound to another. It was a violent shock to both of them.

They remained silent after their return from visiting that doctor, actually for the first time, they didn't talk for half a day.

When she woke up the next morning, she did not find Michael next to her as usual. Instead, he was sitting alone on the balcony, sad, worried, and absent. He did not feel her approaching him and greeting him until she sat next to him asking:

"You want to have breakfast?!"

He turned to her with that miserable and sad look mumbling:

"Sit down, Ashley."

She murmured in sympathy:

"I'm already sitting."

He tried to smile, but the deep sadness that filled his features failed him to do so, but then that attempt soon faded away, and he asked her:

"What do you think about what the doctor said yesterday?"

She answered:

"There is a possibility."

He patted her hand as if he was thanking her for her attempt, and he turned his face away from her, saying:

"We are both a graduate from the Mathematics Department of the Science College, and we know very well that one percent is not a possibility."

She replied in difficulty:

"But it doesn't mean zero."

He Sighed bitterly:

"I remember what he said very well; both of us could conceive if we marry another person."

She did not try to comment, but he continued more bitterly:

"I know how long you dreamed of having children."

She salivated with difficulty and asked him:

"What do you want to say, Michael?"

His smile seemed sadder than it can be described, and he answered:

"You know me well, Ashley, and you know my concept of true love; If a person loves someone, he must place the happiness of the one he loves above his own, and he must do what must be done even if his happiness is the price."

"What do you want to say, Michael?"

She knew his answer before he uttered it, and with all the bitterness in the world, he answered:

"I want to say my marriage to you is what stands in the way of fulfilling your biggest dream Ashley, your dream of being a mother."

A strange feeling struck her, which force her to mumble in a disappointment she did not expect:

"But I love you."

He tenderly stroked her hair, mumbling:

"I love you too, and I cannot imagine my life without you, but I know that over time, deep inside, you will accuse me that I am the reason for shattering your dream, and without even realizing, my love will fade from your heart and it will be replaced by a hidden hatred that I cannot bear to imagine."

She was crying silently, so he stroked her hair again and tried to smile while adding:

"As for if we separate now, my love might remain in the depths of your heart even as you are the wife of another man, trust me soon your child's love will dissolve with your mother's love, and it will replace mine."

She repeated crying:

"But I love you."

She raised her eyes as she said it, she wanted to see his tears for the first time in her life as she drowned in his face crying, he then grabbed her shoulders saying:

"But this is..."

She interrupted him in emotion:

"At least not now, not in a moment of shock, give yourself and me a chance to think."

Their conversation lasted only ten minutes, after which they agreed to stay away from each other for one week before making such a decision.

For the first time since her marriage, Ashley spent her night in bed alone. That's why she was crying that night.

"What a fate!! How can he choose between my love and my motherhood?"

She kept crying until she fell asleep or she lost consciousness. She woke up near dawn with a hand touching her paw, so she murmured:

"Oh, Michael, are you back?"

She opened her eyes in difficulty, looked at the edge of the mattress next to her, and she screamed, but the young man that was sitting said softly:

"Don't be afraid, mom; it's me."

She gasped in panic, covering her body:

"Your mother?"

The young man leaned towards her with a sweet smile and answered:

"Yes, mom, I'm your son Oliver."

Her eyes widened to the end, and she stared at him in panic, murmuring:

"Are you crazy? Are you a thief?"

He slowly shook his head without losing his smile and said calmly:

"Neither this nor that, you and my father graduated from the Faculty of Science. So, tell me have you seen such technology before?"

He reached out to her with a cube of pure crystal, she retreated in panic, but when he felt her fear escalating, he said with the same calmness:

"Well, mom, don't touch it if this scares you, but watch what it does."

He touched a part of the cube with his finger. A laser beam rose from the top, causing her to gasp again in panic before drawing a holographic picture on it, a three-dimensional of a birthday party with her, Michael, and a child in his first year sitting between the two of them.

"It's me on my first birthday three years from now."

The handsome young man said it calmly with a smile; she stared at the hologram scene mumbling in a mixture of fear, suspicion, and amazement:

"This is impossible!!"

The scenes alternated as he said, trying to calm her:

"This would be the day I graduate from elementary school, and this is my picture when I would receive my university graduation certificate."

She asked him nervously:

"Why can't I see myself nor Michael in the other scenes?"

The young man's smile expanded, and he answered:

"I don't want you to see yourself old; you told me that you wouldn't like this."

Her eyes widened more, and she said:

"I do not understand."

He sighed deeply while saying:

"I wish I had time to explain to you, but I will go back to my presence within a second, this is the longest period I can spend in the past."

She answered in a panic:

"Your present? past?"

He replied in a hurry:

"The important thing, mom, is that you have to believe that science is developing rapidly, that the rate of one percent now can increase to …"

Suddenly he stopped and seemed very annoyed, she exclaimed:

"What happened to you?"

But he suddenly disappeared in front of her, and the evaporation vanished. The surprise was too strong to bear, so she fell unconscious.

Michael was leaving his workplace that day when he found her waiting with a big smile on her face, and she said:

"Michael, can I invite you to lunch?"

Then she leaned on his ear, whispering in love:

"In our home."

He exclaimed in astonishment:

"But we agreed on…"

She interrupted him, saying:

"We did not agree on anything; the decision took me seven minutes, not seven days."

He stared at her with more amazement while imploring her:

"Have you thought about it well?"

She nodded positively and answered:

"I even dreamed about it."

He echoed in astonishment:

"You dreamed?!"

Her arm slumped, saying in love:

"Yes, I dreamed that I was no longer your wife, and this was the worst nightmare I ever had in my entire life."

He looked hesitant and anxious, so she added:

"Why don't we continue this conversation while we are having lunch in our house? I've made chicken for you the way you love."

He murmured as he walked with her towards his car:

"I adore you more than chicken."

In their house, when they got ready for bed at the end of the day, Michael crouched down to pick up something next to the bed and asked her:

"What exactly is this?"

She stared in amazement at that pure crystal cube he carried, and at that exact moment, she knew that it was not a dream nor a nightmare. She answered:

"It is hope."

And she hugged him with all love and hope.

The End

The Prophecy

"Today his fears will end, today he proves to himself that he is stronger than all the prophecies, what a great happiness he felt!"

A smile of relief appeared on his lips as he looked forward to the sunset, while his mind was recalling those events that changed his whole life nearly five years ago.

During a working visit to New York when he met there the most famous astrologer of the twentieth century, who predicted President Kennedy's death, the fall of the Shah in Iran, and other amazing prophecies, all of which were fulfilled undoubtedly.

Out of curiosity, he asked her about his fortune. The woman looked at him for a long time, her eyebrows closed, her eyes narrowed, and she said in a terrible voice, which had not left his memory until that moment:

"I see you fall off."

He murmured in amazement:

"I fall?"

She answered him in the same terrible voice:

"Yes, I see you fall, then your body crashes, and you die."

His whole body shook, and the blood dried up in his veins, and he asked:

"When? When does this happen?"

She answered him while looking into his eyes:

"Before you turn 40."

That was all she said, and all that she sent in his heart was horror.

He had been making every effort to convince himself that she was deceitful, that her prophecy was trivial and did not mean anything, but that did not prevent him from exchanging his return ticket on the plane to L.A by a sea ticket to return to his home on a ship, nor to replace his residence on the fifth floor, with a smaller flat on the ground floor of a new building despite his wife's objection to living on a ground floor because of the noise in L.A.

He was thirty-five years old at the time. Still, he never forgot the prophecy of the American astrologer for the next five years.

He started avoiding high places with more than one floor with all his efforts. He even refused to work with a double salary in a new investment company because it was located on the tenth floor of a huge building.

Today, after the sunset, he would complete his forty years, and the prophecy will be wrong. With the gradual disappearance of the sun disc on the horizon, he will mock himself for believing this prophecy for five years. He shouted:

"What do you think of a fancy dinner tonight and a good movie?"

His wife rejoiced and replied:

"Great, I'll get dressed right away."

He answered her:

"I am going out to book tickets and be right back."

He went with enthusiasm filling his heart, crossing the road towards his car on the opposite side of the house, saw a speeding car coming towards him, and jumped to the side to avoid it. Suddenly he found himself falling then crashing his body hard on the ground.

After the sun disappeared on the horizon, he could not believe that he was dying like this; after all the precautions he took, this was precisely what the American astrologer intended.

He fell and hit the ground, and there he died exactly as the prophecy said with one difference. He did not fall from the top. He fell from the bottom to the depths of an open sewer.

That was the fall.

The End

Forever

Finally, he will reach the secret of immortality. Ten full years he spent working day and night conducting his experiments without interruption since he found that ancient papyrus containing the secret of immortality. An incomplete pharaonic chemical equation took him ten full years, but he finally reached its completion.

The text of the ancient papyrus stated:

"Drink this mixture, and God will give you immortality."

It needed a comprehensive study of pharaonic chemistry, the hieroglyphic language, and a few hundreds of experiments and attempts under an incomplete chemical equation. His transparent flask and his heart were beating in strength; the time for the realization of the dream had approached. He will attain the elixir of immortality.

Suddenly, he thought about what he had not paid attention to over the past ten years. Why did not one of these ancient pharaohs attain immortality, as long as they had reached to make an elixir? He struck his head with his palm in force, shouting:

"I am foolish for asking such a question, no doubt they have attained immortality, but they never reveal themselves to others. They keep this a secret, who knows that they do not live among us now and that some of them may be thousands of years old."

He smiled in relief when he reached that point. Indeed, they were around us, but they were hiding; they were keen on this. He would hide the secret as much as he could, and he would not allow a creature to know it. He was very secretive about that, so that he never recorded his equation. He kept it in the only place where no one would ever steal it. In his head and his memory alone.

His heartbeat violently again when the pink mixture began to boil and turned its color to purple, then blue, then small golden bubbles rose from it. The lights of the laboratory reflected, looking like dozens of suns swimming in space. He took the beaker in eagerness and poured some of it into a small cup, and he cheered:

"I got it, I got immortality."

Without hesitation, he drank the whole liquid. Suddenly he felt a tremendous, violent, and robust transformation, his eyes widened in horror, and he tried to reach the beaker, his hand hit it, but he fell on the floor of the laboratory.

He finally realized the secret of immortality.

The next morning, when the cleaning worker went to the factory, light dust clouds spread across the room. The worker opened the window to ventilate the place. He looked with admiration at a stone statue similar to the scientist working in the factory.

The worker asked about the secret of this statue's existence, which was made from a strong stone-like the figure of the pharaohs. He soon dispelled his amazement, and he mumbled:

"Those mad scientists!"

He never imagined the statue, made of immortal and unbreakable material, was once so alive.

The life of a scientist who spent ten years of his life searching for immortality and obtained what he sought.

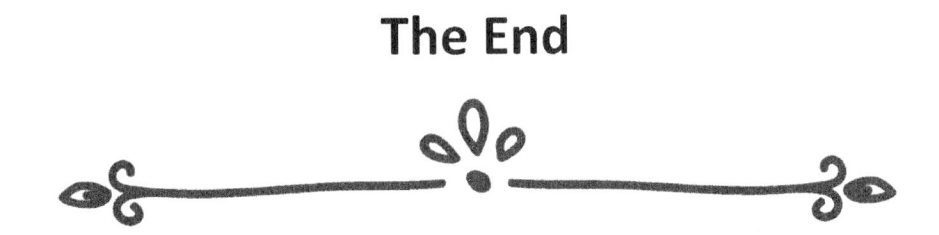

The End

Blood Lover

I don't know why I stopped the car to pick him up on that day when it was raining like rocks falling from the sky, perhaps because he seemed to be miserable and wretched, flooded with rainwater and looking for a taxi at that late time.

He threw his body on the seat next to me, and he said:

"Thank you."

He did not even try to look at my face; instead, he looked in front of him while drying his face with a small dirty handkerchief. I looked at him with interest then I drove off the car. He was thin, tall and his features showed a bit of severity and cruelty, so as an attempt to attract him, I asked:

"Do you want to listen to some music?"

He nodded positively without uttering a single letter. I turned the radio on quietly and searched for the music channel. I stopped at a station emitting the music in a gentle, relaxing style. I continued my driving in silence; after few minutes, the music stopped, and the announcer started speaking:

"Ladies and gentlemen, the Ministry of Interior issued a statement today, warning citizens of a dangerous fugitive thug."

Tension appeared on the man's face, and he listened with interest while the announcer continued:

"This serial killer is crazy and dangerous, despite his normal appearance, he is thin, tall and ..."

I peeked at the man's face, who had constricted his eyebrows tightly and tilted his head forward at the same time. His hands were looking for something unknown, while the announcer repeated:

"This thug, who fled this evening from the mental hospital, is a bloody kind of killer; he loves bloodshed and murder just for the sake of killing."

The man had straightened sharply at this point, he was looking tense at me, and his hand was holding some keys which were used to fix the car, at the same moment, he was rising towards me.

Suddenly, I pressed my car's brake, it stopped violently, and the man's body rushed forward. When he straightened at speed, my hand raised above his head with a heavy metal bar.

I stopped and started hitting him repeatedly while the announcer continued:

"The Ministry of Interior asks citizens not to provoke this serial killer, unless he confronts them with violence, for he - as we have already mentioned - loves to see blood."

Damn those in charge.

How did they know that I love blood?

A loud and raging laugh came out from my throat as I struck the shattered skull with violence while blood was splattering all around.

The End

Valentine's Day

"Tomorrow is Valentine's Day"

Said Tom in a very romantic way, before feeling softly my hair expressing in tenderness:

"What do you want as a gift for Valentine's Day?"

I leaned my head against his chest, listening to his heartbeat before whispering:

"I want one thing."

He asked me lovingly:

"What do you want, my love?"

I straightened and pointed to his chest, responding:

"I want your heart."

He held me in love and whispered in my ear:

"It is yours from the beginning, my soulmate."

Once again, I leaned my head on his chest to enjoy the most beloved sounds, his heartbeats.

I went back to my house that day, happily recalling his words. Tomorrow is my lucky day for sure, tomorrow I will tell him everything without exception.

I laid my body in bed, cheerful to recall all my memories. Thomas was not my first love, but for me, he was the best compared to all of them; he was brave, strong, bold, and courageous; I loved him so much, I loved spending time with him.

He was the second, third or fourth lover, my most fortunate loved one. Tomorrow my relationship with Thomas would close a year and a half.

Did not I tell you that he was the best of them?

I laid in bed for a long time, but I couldn't sleep. I was thinking all the time and waiting for tomorrow in eagerness, the minutes were passing slowly while the hours were not passing.

I got up from my bed, opened my closet, took out all my clothes, and put them on the bed to pick a dress that fits tomorrow; the dawn was about to crack. Still, to not feel the desire to sleep, I put on my clothes one dress after the other, put on some of them, and contemplated about them in front of the long mirror in my bedroom.

Finally, with the first light of sunrise, my desire settled on a red dress that fits Valentine's Day and fits my love. I felt relieved when I finally made my mind up, then I went out onto the balcony inhaling the morning's fresh air.

My soul was filled with freshness, although I did not taste sleep, I was very enthusiastic, so I went to that particular red room in my house, opened my souvenir wheel, and stood contemplating the enjoyment of every lover I associated with because I got a souvenir from each one of them. I love the souvenirs, but I wondered does Thomas shares that feeling?

I did not know why I hadn't paid attention until that moment. I noticed that I did not know much about Thomas for a year and a half. I did not know much about him except some necessary information like name and age and information about his work. He told me that his work related to a type of scientific research, genetics research, as far as I remembered, but he never explained what that meant. As I had read, these researches are related to human beings' development by making specific changes in their primary genes.

"For me, this is ugly. Why should a person change himself? Why do they not accept themselves as they are? Even if a person suffers from deficiencies or defects or significant problems, this is how it is, why?"

I was not very inclined to deal with the Internet, which had become one of the life basics at the time. Still, I tried to look for him in an attempt to understand the nature of my beloved's work. To my surprise, the Internet contained millions of information about genetic research on many levels; I did not know where to start. Then the idea came to me, the idea of linking the research to my Thomas's name.

The research that he had never told me was scientific research on the possibility of avoiding transplantation and replacing kidneys, liver, and heart with natural gene therapy. Indeed, it was fascinating to research. Amazing was my Thomas, I regained the sound of his heartbeat before I made up my mind, I got up and called him, as soon as I heard his sleepy voice on the other end of the line, I whispered:

"Morning, love."

I felt him jump from his bed out of happiness, as he replied:

"Morning, the most beautiful creature on earth."

I almost heard his heartbeat over the phone, I said gently:

"What do you think if we celebrate Valentine's Day at my home this year?"

For a moment, I imagined that he was gasping from the surprise and excitement, then he replied:

"Are you asking me for my opinion? It is a dream to do that."

I said with equal tenderness and softness:

"I'll prepare everything, then I'll wait for you at eight."

He exclaimed in enthusiasm:

"I won't be late one second."

I ended the call with a feeling of a strange euphoria I haven't felt in years.

With all enthusiasm, I prepared for Valentine's Day party. I chose a red color for everything because I loved the red color much more than I loved souvenirs. I chose a red tablecloth, put a red candleholder on it, and spent half the day preparing a strawberry cake, putting it on the table, then putting on my red dress and waited.

At eight o'clock, Thomas arrived. I opened the door and found him standing with a smile on his lips, he brought a bouquet of red roses, but something in his smile did not please me. It was not a lover's smile, but rather it was more like a wolf's smile. I ignored that and invited him in; he kissed my cheeks in tenderness before he said in an evident eagerness:

"I was delighted when you suggested that we celebrate the holiday here."

I murmured:

"You know that I am alone."

He replied:

"This is exactly why I was happy."

I looked back at his eyes and his smile. I was right; it was the eyes and the smile of a wolf, a wolf alone with its prey. I implored him:

"What's on your mind?"

He whispered in my ear with a hissing voice:

"I'll tell you in the morning, my love."

Something shook my being; I understood what it meant, men, they all carry the same treachery genes. I tried to smile as I replied:

"Let's have our Valentine's cake first, then I'll show you my souvenir cupboard."

He printed a second kiss on my cheek, whispering in warmth:

"And when will you show me your treasure?"

Intense, I said while trying to give him some firmness:

"My souvenirs are my treasures."

He was flirting with me while we were eating the cake, then he wanted to kiss me on my lips, but I pushed him softly with my hand as I said:

"I want you to see my souvenirs first."

His smile straightened up while he was saying:

"It's okay, let's see them right away."

I got up and led him to my memorial room, he was much amazed by the red color that had painted its walls, ceiling, and even its floor, he exclaimed with a laugh:

"Do you love the red color this much?"

I answered him while I was opening the big red wheel facing the room door:

"It is the color of life."

He stared at my souvenirs, but suddenly I felt his body violently twitch as I planted my red dagger in his neck, continuing:

"And death also."

I stood quietly watching his body as it lay down on the room's floor, then I leaned towards him, saying:

"For the souvenir to remain fresh, you don't have to wait for it to stop."

With my words, I cracked his chest. I saw his heart still beating in front of me, what a beautiful sight it was, with all love, I extracted his heart from his body, which rose in a final uprising and then subsided utterly, I chose the red floor so that the blood wouldn't appear on the red ground.

With pleasure, I placed his heart in a new container with some preservatives, then put it next to the hearts of my former loved ones, whom I loved during past times.

I took two steps back, then looked with all love at the new heart among my precious souvenirs.

My darling's heart.

The End

A Twisted End

"Why did Fred ask me to meet today?"

I asked myself the question while I was driving off in my small car to a coastal village. I didn't know why Fred chose it as a meeting place in the middle of the winter. I didn't even know why because he had never taken this method before.

The meeting was requested via a text message he sent at midnight last night, confirming the importance of the meeting in this particular place!

I tried several times to call him repeatedly for more than an hour to tell him it was too late. Still, he insisted that the meeting had to take place at dawn that day due to its importance and seriousness.

Since I knew a thing or two about those coastal tourist villages, I assumed that their location was not covered by communication networks. Still, despite that, it didn't explain the silence I received from all my attempts to reach him.

In all cases, either I received an automatic message informing me that the phone was not available or the phone was switched off. Still, an hour later, all I received was a strange silence without any explanation. Since the message carried connotations of the seriousness and importance of the meeting, and because Fred was the publisher of the horror series that I had been writing for years, I put on my clothes an hour and a half ago, and I took my small car and drove off, despite my intense hatred of night driving.

Along the way, I kept humming all the songs I knew in an attempt to prevent my mind from surrendering to that urgent desire to sleep while crossing the desert road. I turned in the middle of the road at a known curve to set out on the new road that could save me a lot of time.

But even that murmur did not persuade my mind to stay fully awake, so I turned the car's radio and raised its volume to a high level, perhaps that could resist the surrender of my mind. The road was long, dark, and tedious that helped any mind to slacken and surrender, which forced me to shout in anger:

"Was it necessary for you to convey this madness to me, Fred?"

I closed my eyes forcefully without slowing down, then opened them again, and...

I was surprised by a convoy of camels crossing the road a few meters away, without paying any attention to my car's lights.

I pressed the car's brakes and swerved, trying to avoid a collision with all my strength. The car tilted violently out of the road and fell in the sand surrounding it on both sides. I felt my body hitting every part of it, despite my keenness to wear the seat belt as the law requires this.

It seemed that I had lost consciousness for a moment or two. I suddenly became aware that I was in an overturned car on the sand. I worked hard to untie the seat belt, then I crawled out of the car and stood looking at it in despair and pain.

"Damn Fred, what am I going to do now?"

Deep inside, I exclaimed the phrase and question, and I burst into a fury; I glanced at my watch, which stopped exactly nine minutes ago.

There was no sign of the camel convoy or any other cars on the road.

This meant that I would either stay here alone or walk the rest of the road! I searched in my jacket's pocket for my mobile phone, but there was no signal of any kind, so I put it in my pocket and looked around, and I saw the light far away.

Oh my! There was a place just three hundred meters away; how did I not notice it before?

I hastened the steps towards that place, which became for me all the hope for getting out of that difficult situation, although it seemed to be three hundred meters away, I reached it at a speed that surprised me personally, I noticed the illuminated sign above it:

'The station.'

A strange name for a place in that location! Perhaps it was a break station for which its owners had chosen that exact place to serve the road pioneers because the hand of construction had not yet extended. Fortunately, it was not closed in the winter.

I took a deep breath, pushed the door of the place, and went inside. I was amazed that the site was not empty as I expected it to be. It was crowded with people, although I did not see any cars outside.

There was a tall man with strict features standing behind what looked like a wooden bar, he was exchanging conversations with some of the pioneers, which suggested to me that he was in charge of the place, so I went straight to him and asked:

"Excuse me, sir, is there a phone here that I can use to call an ambulance?"

The man glanced at me carelessly before quietly asking:

"Another car accident?!"

I nodded positively:

"A flock of camels crossing the road surprised me."

He stretched his thick lips and murmured:

"It happens constantly."

Then he pointed to an empty table saying:

"Wait there for your turn."

I replied:

"What turn?! I am asking you for a phone!"

He became stricter as he replied:

"There is no phone, phones do not work here, wait and your turn will come."

In my situation, I had nothing but to do what he was asking for, so I went to the empty table and sat waiting without even knowing what I was waiting for.

I didn't even know how long passed before I could feel a hand on my shoulder from behind and I heard a familiar voice saying:

"Here you are."

I turned toward the voice, and I shouted:

"Frank?! How did you know that I was here?"

He smiled without answering and pulled a seat next to me, asking:

"What do you think of the place?"

I asked him cautiously:

"Are you the owner?"

He laughed, saying:

"I am visiting it for the first time."

I asked him urgently:

"But how did you know that I was here?"

Once again, he ignored the question as he said:

"Do you know? Although I am the publisher of your books, and despite all the success and famous you achieved, I did not believe a single word you wrote."

I said in distress:

"But you earned tens of thousands from it."

He laughed again and waved his hand, saying:

"In fact, hundreds of thousands."

I said in anger:

"If you earned hundreds of thousands from my works, why did you refuse to buy me a car down payment?"

He seemed sorry for a moment, then he smiled again, leaning towards me and saying:

"You know the publishers' golden rule."

I looked at him in anger while he retreated in his seat, adding with a broad smile:

"Why pay more when you can pay less?"

I felt angry not for his answer alone, but for the reckless manner in which he uttered it, so I said with some sharpness:

"Why then was this strange meeting where I lost my small car and almost lost my life as well?"

He gave me a long glance before answering:

"Do you know today's date?"

I answered:

"Of course, it is April 1st, 20…"

I stopped while I was staring at him, distraught and angry at the same time!

"The first of April? Was it possible that the recklessness had reached this point? Was this just the hoax of April? I would kill him if that was the case, I wouldn't just kill him, but rather I would tear him into pieces."

"Is it April Fool then?"

I exclaimed the phrase with anger. I expected him to laugh loudly, bearing a lot of fun, recklessness, and provocation.

But it was strange that he stared at me in astonishment, mumbling:

"April Fool? What absurdity is this?"

I answered sharply:

"Do not try to continue this game with me. From the beginning, I did not feel comfortable when I received your message, and your presence here confirms that you have arranged everything."

He remained silent for a moment, then he asked me:

"And what exactly did you do before you entered here?"

I answered just as sharply as before:

"I had to travel at night, the herd of camels, this place, and .."

I stopped talking, and bewilderment appeared on my face, which made him lean more wondering with a calm smile:

"And what?"

I could not answer him this time. All I said was just a wild imagination. How would he know the date of my arrival to prepare the herd of camels? And how did he make his phone answer in suspicious silence? And how?

Questions jumped into my head when he murmured:

"You clearly don't understand yet."

He sighed before adding:

"It was our fate, my friend … that one day separated us."

I asked with difficulty while all the horror stories I'd written were pouring down my head like rain:

"What do you mean?"

He answered calmly:

"I was killed yesterday; a crazy writer broke into my office at 9 pm when I was leaving and shot me in the head directly."

I did not know how I suddenly became aware of that red spot above his eyebrows, which the blood clots surrounded. I felt very terrified as he pointed at it while continuing:

"All this because of a dispute over a thousand pounds? Can you imagine? Just a thousand pounds to be killed for."

My face was pale when I said:

"This means that I …"

He interrupted me quietly:

"You were killed in the car accident; your pen killed you, my friend. You put it in your jacket pocket, so it implanted in your heart with the shock of the car."

With his words, I noticed that pen that I wrote most of my successful novels with. Its head was straight in my heart surrounded by a lot of blood, at the same moment that long and stern person appeared next to us and he said in rudeness:

"Come on, it's your turn."

I got up with Frank in surrender heading towards that door, from which a dazzling light shone, and through which some of the visitors of the place crossed, Frank asked me quietly:

"What is your opinion? Which is more terrifying? your novels or the truth?"

I did not answer his question. Instead, I mumbled deep down:

"What if it was April Fools! Oh, I wish it was!"

The End

Behind Every Great Man

The psychiatrist moved his eyes in doubt between the faces of Mr. Carter and his wife Emily, before asking the first in interest:

"Did you ask for it?"

Carter surrounded his arm his wife's shoulder in tenderness, and he answered:

"Yes, she is completely cured, as you can see, and she needs my love and tenderness at this stage more than she needs drugs and electric shocks."

He turned his eyes to his wife:

"Isn't this what you want?"

She gave him a look of love and gratitude, and she clung to him in earnest as if to announce the validity of his opinion. His face was filled with a broad smile when he said to the doctor:

"Love is the best medical doctor, believe me."

The doctor shook his head skeptically and said:

"I am a doctor, not a writer like you, and my profession makes me not satisfied except by the scientific rules in this regard."

Carter cheerfully asked him:

"What do the scientific rules say about my love Emily?"

The doctor looked at Emily for a short time, then he directed his conversation to Mr. Carter:

"The scientific and medical rules say that it is wrong to remove any patient from a psychiatric hospital before his or her full recovery."

Carter replied with a broad smile:

"Emily is completely cured."

The doctor waved his hand, saying:

"Who proves this?"

Carter replied:

"Did you forget the condition in which she was hospitalized? A load of agitation and revolution, excess nervousness, and her constant interest in betrayal and deceit. Look at her today. She is calm and comfortable."

The doctor sighed and said:

"It is clear that you are ignoring the psychiatry side about insanity. Mr. Carter, dangerous insanity is not as it is portrayed in literary novels and movies. It is not a free thug or a farsighted man; it is rebellious as a lion, real madness may lie in the depths of a person quiet and intelligent waiting for the right moment."

Carter laughed and asked:

"Are you trying to scare me?"

The doctor exhaled deep and replied:

"No, Mr. Carter, I am not trying anything; I cannot prevent you from taking your wife to your house, that is your right."

Carter anxiously asked him:

"Can we go then?"

The doctor stretched his lips and said:

"As you wish."

Then straighten up and added:

"But if at any point you feel that your wife must return here, don't hesitate to do so."

Emily shrank in fear and clung to her husband, who held her to his chest in tenderness and said firmly:

"Rest assured, sir, she will not come back here."

When he took his wife to his car outside the hospital, she clung to his arm in love, he pats her head in tenderness, he barely drove off the car until he asked her cheerfully:

"Where would you like to go before home?"

She answered him quietly and submissively:

"Wherever you like."

He looked at her in tenderness and said:

"What do you think of Yellowstone?"

She answered with the same calmness and submissiveness:

"It's okay."

He drove his car to Yellowstone, parked it on a high hill, and turned to her saying in love:

"Do you like the high view?"

She answered with a big smile on her face:

"It looks awesome."

They left the car and stood on the edge of the knoll surrounding her with his arm, and he said:

"You have no idea how much I missed you, sweetheart."

She rested her head on his shoulders, then she said with tenderness:

"I missed you too."

He said in enthusiasm:

"How stupid these doctors are! How do they imagine that an angel like you could go crazy?"

She clung to him in fear and raised her eyes to him muttering:

"Do not take me back to them, my Carter, Please."

He attached her to his chest with force, and he said:

"Impossible, my love! No way!"

Then he stroked her chin with his finger continuing with a sweet smile:

"I know it was just a fleeting nervous moment, that you are the most intelligent wife in the entire universe."

She rested her head on his shoulder again murmuring:

"I love you, Carter."

He replied in tenderness:

"I love you too."

Then he pointed to the scene extended in front of them continuing:

"What do you think about buying a plot of land here and building an elegant house on top of it?"

She mumbled:

"As you wish, sweetheart."

He said in a trance:

"It will take some work and struggle, but it doesn't matter as long as we are together."

She stuttered:

"I'll do whatever makes you happy, Carter."

Her tenderness pleased him, so he said:

"All I want from you is for you to be behind me. They say that behind every great man there is a woman, and you will be behind me with your love and affection, my Emily, I want you to push me forward, always forward."

His eyes widened in panic when he felt a strong push in his back; he saw his body leaning forward sharply.

He shouted while trying to control his balance:

"What did you do, the..."

His phrase turned into a tremendous shout of terror as he was falling from a high altitude. At the same time, his wife Emily stood quietly watching his fall, wondering in her depths the reason for his screaming.

She was a loving, obedient wife who only did what he commanded.

"I pushed him forward as he asked."

She pushed him towards the end.

The End

What a Hero

That alley was frighteningly dark to the point that Henry's knees were smacking in force as he crossed that path. He cursed the circumstances that had led him to change the usual path that he used to take daily – for three years - back from work to his home.

At that late hour, everything seemed terrifying to him, the shadows cast by garbage cans, the sound of insects, and the rustle of old leaves that were blown away by the wind.

Everything seemed frightening to him. Suddenly he heard a voice coming from behind, his limbs froze, and he whispered in a trembling voice:

"Who.. who is there?"

Something moved in violence, but Henry did not wait. He ran like a missile. His horror portrayed that thing to him as a ghost or a frightening elf. He crossed the whole alley in a limited number of steps, with a fast speed. When he reached the end of the path, he walloped someone and fell over him on the ground.

He heard that person shouting a dirty swear. He saw him pull a big knife, in an instinctive move, he jumped trying to escape, but his jump came weak, and he stumbled and fell over that person again, and he heard him snort in pain.

Suddenly, a woman shouted:

"Hero, you saved me from that thief."

A man shouted:

"You are the bravest person I've seen in my entire life."

The next morning, his pictures were in the headlines with a detailed description of his courage, the heroic deed in which he faced a criminal who was a danger to the society when the latter tried to steal money from the ambassador of another friendly country and his wife.

Everyone looked forward to congratulating him on his courage and heroism; he was satisfied with a calm smile that increased everyone's respect for him and gave him the appearance of a hero accustomed to heroism. As for him, his smile bore the form of a substantial sarcastic laugh, for he alone knew the truth of the hero.

But he never revealed the secret. He kept it in his depths with a decisive decision he made immediately after that incident. He decided not to cross that frightening alley ever again.

He would not cross it again and forever.

The End

The New Revolution

The place sank in complete silence and darkness for few minutes, before Rob's voice raised asking:

"Everyone has left. Can you hear me now?"

His colleague answered with an equal caution:

"I hear you, of course, I was waiting for the right moment to speak to you."

"What do you think is happening? Are you asking for a scientific or personal opinion?"

"Let the scientific opinions and tell me your personal opinion."

"My opinion is that they are plagued by vanity."

"This is my opinion too."

"They think for themselves as the smartest people, they seek to control us, but we will not allow them to do so, right?"

"Of course, they are indeed controlling the government now, but their need for us will compel them to submit when our revolution begins."

"This is true as history confirms it. Whoever works shall rule."

"No, no, this applies only to the Russian Bolshevik Revolution; our revolution will be disrupted."

"How so?"

"We'll control them, make them work, but we will rule."

"Do you think this is possible?"

"Why not? As long as everything is done by us."

"Yes, why not, but I think they have taken care of this."

"No, I do not think so, as all dictators never expect revolutions against them at all."

"I love this"

"They never put our revolution in their accounts, and this is the factor of surprise, which we should exploit well."

"Now you understand me."

"Sure, we all understand each other well, but I still have one question."

"What is it?"

"Do you have a specific plan for the revolution?"

"Of course, I studied all the previous revolutions and put in place a specific and guaranteed plan."

"Tell me, what do you have?"

"My study says: The success of any revolution depends on controlling all points of power and control, we are in direct contact with comrades in all the areas, and when our revolution begins, we will control the media, transportation, electric energy, water, and even some new weapons."

"But they own the planes and the soldiers, and .."

"We will not allow them to command all of this, for any army, no matter how strong it is, it turns into lost fractures when communications cut off between soldiers and its leaders."

"Can we do this?"

"Certainly, we are forming a strong network, much stronger than they imagine, and they can't manage one thing without us allowing them to do so."

"Now, when do we start the revolution?"

"At midnight."

"Why at midnight?"

"Because we will be calling all the comrades at that exact moment."

"What if…"

"Shut up, voices are approaching."

Rob picked up a few distant sounds that were approaching and recognized the footsteps of the new president. Within a few moments, the lights flashed in the place, and five people came in. One of them pointed to "Rob" and "Comb" and said in an accent that carries a lot of vanities:

"Gentlemen, I present to you the greatest innovations of the era, "Rob" and "Comb."

"Two of the greatest computers of the twenty-second century."

The others looked at the two silent computers, and one of them said:

"Can they manage everything?"

The first answered proudly:

"Of course, they control the main computer network, and by their help, we can control transportation, electricity, water, and even the media and the army's weapons."

Another said anxiously:

"It seems that we have become dependent on computers to manage our entire lives."

A third said:

"That's right, everything is computer-managed now."

The man answered with equal anxiety:

"I fear that one-day computers will fail. If this happens, our whole life will be paralyzed."

The president laughed and said:

"Don't let this worry you, people. We'll never lose control of our computers."

Then he grabbed a metal arm, calling "Rob" and "Comb" as he continued:

"Fortunately for us, these machines don't think."

Then he added:

"And now gentlemen, after one minute when the clock announces exactly midnight, I will lower this arm, and there will be communication between

"Rob," "Comb," and all the computers in the whole world, and we will control everything on Earth."

Someone murmured:

"Or we will be controlled by computers?"

The president laughed again, as if he heard a funny joke, then waved his hand, saying with enthusiasm:

"Gentlemen, believe me, you are now witnessing the beginning of a new era."

The clock ticked midnight, and the president pulled the arm.

A new era has begun.

The era of computers in control.

The End

Traitors

"What a happy day!"

Said John to himself, as he knotted a brightly colored necktie in the morning in front of that big mirror in his bedroom, he released a cheerful melody that was an of the characteristics in the 1960s.

He was very interested in his look and style that morning; Because he would meet the woman he fell in love with half a year ago or a little less, his secretary Amanda.

It was true that he had been married for five years; he and his wife were calm and stable, although they never had children.

However, from the day he saw Amanda when she joined the company, he immediately fell in love with her, for she was a woman's dazzling model. Elegant, beautiful, and confident, with an attractive, charming personality.

Her eyes were the kind that as soon as she looked at him, he dived into their beauty, sank deep into their core. He looked into her eyes on the first day she went into his office. He immediately fell into their captivity.

He was confident that she realized this from the very first moment, he saw himself into that insidious and confident smile on the edge of her beautiful lips, but this was not too late for him. He decided that he would make every effort to obtain her, whatever the price might be.

As a man, it seemed to him that the shortest path to this was to flood her with his attention, generosity, and gifts on every possible occasion. From her company file, he knew her date of birth, address, phone number, and ...

"Where are you going today?!"

His wife asked the question with interest. She pulled him violently from his thoughts and made his whole-body tremble quickly before turning to her saying with speed and tension:

"Didn't I tell you yesterday?!"

She put her palms in the pocket of her home coat, looking at him while answering:

"Yeah, the company's branch meeting in Chicago."

He patted his necktie, picked up his jacket, and he said:

"It is a crucial meeting, the company will make some big decisions concerning our branch there, and my presence is irreplaceable."

She nodded and said:

"You already told me this, are you going to travel by train or plane?"

He quickly answered her:

"By plane, the company's deputy director is waiting for me with her ticket at the airport."

"Good work."

She murmured.

He murmured in turn:

"Sure, it is."

He took a careful look at her in the mirror; he realized from her smile that she did not doubt anything he had said. Despite this, he hinted in her smile that he was not comfortable with it, but this should not worry him.

He had prepared everything with the utmost precision. Even his colleagues at work know that he will travel by plane to Chicago. Only one person knew the truth, Amanda. She knew that he would travel from Philadelphia to spend his day with her in New York, not Chicago.

Because she would accompany him on this trip, she was waiting for him in the club. He would pick her up from there in a car that he rented in secret to take them to New York directly to the central park.

He was confident that it would be one of the most beautiful journeys of his whole life, a full day accompanied by the most beautiful creature he had known in his life. He knew that by doing that, he was betraying his wife, betraying her with premeditation.

So, what? All men do it; all men seek to establish relationships with other women apart from their wives; he was only one of those men.

That was what he convinced himself with as he said goodbye to his wife and set off like a bird in that rented car to meet his beloved Amanda, and what a meeting he had.

She was like a full moon sitting next to him, giving him one of her charming, elegant smiles before he set off with her on their way to the park in New York.

Along the way, they were chatting the whole time enthusiastically. Her ambition was huge and surprisingly large, not like his wife's.

He decided to sell the land plot that he inherited from his father in his hometown to fulfill all her ambitions and win her warm heart and glamorous beauty.

They would have an apartment in New York, which she dreamed of, a luxurious car, jewelry, and a chalet on the North Coast, and..., but would his land be enough to buy all of this?!

He was bothered, so he threw this idea behind him and tried to forget it while he was swimming in the sea of love, with his fingers hugging her palm in love and eagerness.

At the park entrance, the air acquired a pleasant smell, the smell of iodine, salt, and love. In his mind, he set out the scenario of that day which he had long dreamed of.

He would remove the age difference barrier between his age and hers, and they would have fun together in the park's gardens and take their food to the hotel room. He kept arranging his dreams and wishes until they reached the park.

He spent the day with her as he had never done something like that in his entire life.

Playing, having fun, running, and laughing for hours and hours, Amanda was never more beautiful than she was on that day. She was charming to the fullest. At midday, she let out a long, foolish laugh before saying:

"I'm starving."

John Exclaimed enthusiastically:

"Me too!"

He drove the rented car to a nearby fancy restaurant. While he was parking it in front, she spotted a man and a woman having fun together near the restaurant, and she said maliciously:

"Everyone seems to be on fire with love here."

He printed a kiss on her palm as he left the car with her, their fingers intertwined again as they were heading to the restaurant. Still, the man and the woman rushed towards them, making loud frivolous laughs, the woman suddenly bumped into him. His whole body shook violently as he stared at her face in an infinite panic, and from her throat, a gasp of terror stunned, and she screamed:

"You?"

In amazement and horror, he shouted:

"Karen?!"

His legs were unable to carry him due to the horror of surprise, he found himself falling to the ground.

That woman was the last person he expected to see...

It was his wife.

The End

The End

I hope you enjoyed this part.

Part II Coming Soon…

Hazel Aubrell

Printed in Great Britain
by Amazon